PIRATES of the CARIBBEAN
AT WORLD'S END

THE MYSTIC'S JOURNEY

Adapted by T.T. Sutherland

Based on the screenplay written by Ted Elliott & Terry Rossio

Based on characters created by Ted Elliott & Terry Rossio
and Stuart Beattie and Jay Wolpert

Based on Walt Disney's Pirates of the Caribbean

Produced by Jerry Bruckheimer

Directed by Gore Verbinski

First Edition
1 3 5 7 9 10 8 6 4 2
Library of Congress Catalog Card Number
ISBN-13: 978-1-4231-0380-6
ISBN-10: 1-4231-0380-7

DISNEY PRESS
New York

Chapter 1

Deep in a swamp, up the Pantano River, lived a woman named Tia Dalma.

Tia Dalma was a powerful mystic. She could work strong magic. She was very wise. No one knew where she came from. It seemed like she had always been there.

Tia Dalma was a good person to ask for help. Captain Jack Sparrow knew this. She had helped him before. That was why he went to see her when Davy Jones was after him.

Why was Jones after Jack? Jack was in debt to him. He was supposed to join Jones's crew on the *Flying Dutchman*.

Jack did not want to. He was a captain!
So what could he do?

Jack needed to find a special key. The
key would unlock a chest. Inside this chest
was the heart of Davy Jones. Jack could
control Davy Jones with the heart. Then
Jones would stop chasing him. Jack would
be safe.

Tia Dalma told Jack that Davy Jones
kept the key with him at all times. Then
she gave him a jar full of dirt.

"Davy Jones cannot step on land," Tia
Dalma said. "Land is where you are safe,
and so you will carry land with you."

But the plan failed. Jones sent his pet, a sea beast called the Kraken, to find Jack. The Kraken destroyed many ships. Then, it dragged Jack and his ship, the *Black Pearl*, to the bottom of Davy Jones's Locker.

Jack's crew got away. But they were sad.
They could not believe Jack Sparrow was
gone forever. They wanted to go to Davy
Jones's Locker and rescue him.

So Will Turner, Elizabeth Swann, and
the rest of Jack's crew went to see Tia
Dalma. They knew she had helped Jack.
Maybe she would help him again.

Chapter 2

Tia Dalma said there was a way to bring Jack Sparrow back from the dead. But to do so, they would need help from an old enemy . . . the pirate Barbossa.

Jack and Barbossa did not get along. Jack had killed Barbossa on the Island of the Dead. But Tia Dalma had brought Barbossa back to life. Now Barbossa would help them rescue Jack because Tia Dalma had asked him to.

To save Jack, Barbossa, Will, Elizabeth, and Tia Dalma first had to go to Singapore. They needed a map to World's End—and beyond. The Pirate Lord of Singapore, Captain Sao Feng, had this map. Will was going to steal it.

But they also needed a ship. So
Barbossa and Elizabeth planned to go to
Sao Feng's hideout—a bathhouse—and
ask for one.

This was very dangerous. If Sao Feng
got angry, Barbossa and Elizabeth would
be trapped inside with no weapons. They
would be surrounded by Sao Feng's men.
They would not be able to fight back.

So Jack's crew sneaked into the tunnels underneath the bathhouse. If anything went wrong, the pirates would be there to help. They would have swords and pistols. It would be a fair fight.

The tunnels were in the water below the docks. And they were guarded by East India Trading Company agents. The agents were the sworn enemy of any and all pirates.

The pirates swam silently up to the entrance. They groaned. The entrance had metal bars across it!

How could the pirates saw through the bars? Two agents were standing up above. The agents would hear the noise and catch them. Luckily, Tia Dalma was there to help.

Chapter 3

Squeak squeak squeak . . .

What was that? The agents looked around.

It was only an old woman. She was pushing a cart with squeaky wheels. The cart was full of noisy birds in birdcages.

It was Tia Dalma! The noise of the cart hid the noise from below as the pirates sawed through the bars. They got into the tunnels safely.

And it was lucky they did! Sao Feng had caught Will trying to steal the map!

"You come into my city and you betray me," Sao Feng shouted.

Will, Elizabeth, and Barbossa tried to explain.

Then the bathhouse was attacked!
East India Trading Company agents
burst through the door and windows. All
the pirates turned to fight them together.

Jack's crew came up from the tunnels to help. They were all able to escape. And Will got a ship and the maps from Sao Feng.

They were on their way to World's End!

The ship sailed through icy waters. Sao Feng's maps were strange. They were full of riddles—just like Tia Dalma's magic.

"There be something on the seas that even the most bloodthirsty pirates have come to fear," Tia Dalma told Elizabeth.

Time passed. They were getting closer and closer to World's End.

It was time for Tia Dalma to help Jack . . . again.

So Tia Dalma said some magic words. Then she waited.

Meanwhile, the ship arrived at World's End. It was a giant waterfall that went down and down into darkness. But Tia Dalma was not afraid. She knew where they were going.

Suddenly, the ship plunged over World's
End. Beyond lay Davy Jones's Locker . . .
and Jack Sparrow.

Chapter 4

Everyone survived the fall. They had reached Davy Jones's Locker. But the ship was wrecked.

"We are trapped here," Will said. "No different than Jack."

"Witty Jack be closer than you think," Tia Dalma said. She looked at the horizon. The others looked, too. It was a sail! The *Black Pearl* was moving across the desert!

How did this happen?

Tia Dalma, of course. To help Jack, she had sent thousands of crabs. They had lifted the *Pearl* with their claws and then carried it across the sand. Now they brought Jack and the *Pearl* right to Tia Dalma.

Jack was very happy to see everyone.

"Tia Dalma, out and about!" Jack cried. "How nice of you to come."

After Jack had said his hellos, the *Pearl* sailed off. They were on their way home— if they could *find* their way.

But they had to do it before sunset, warned Tia Dalma. If the ship did not escape the world of the dead by then . . . they would be trapped there forever.

Tia Dalma was sure they would escape. They would get back.

Why was Tia Dalma so sure they would
get back?

She had her own secret reason. She
needed to bring Jack back to the world of
the living. But her reason would have to
stay hidden . . . for now.